by Michael Dahl

art by Migy

ANOTHER
MOUTH
TO FEED

PICTURE WINDOW BOOKS
a capstone imprint

It was on a Tuesday when Harvey
first heard the frightening news.

His mother and father were talking about the
new baby that would soon join the family.

"I can hardly wait for the little monster," said Harvey's mother.

Harvey's father laughed.

"Ah yes, another mouth to feed," he said.

Another **mouth** to feed?

thought Harvey.

Harvey knew what would happen.

His mother would come home from the hospital
with a squirming little creature in her arms.

"Come and look at the new baby,"
his mother would say.

"Isn't he cute?" his father would say.

The mouth baby would lick its lips.

It would CHOMP its bright, sharp teeth.

CHOMP! The dinner table would disappear.

CHOMP! The mouth would eat all of Harvey's toys.

OH NO!

where is the cat?

The mouth would grow bigger and bigger with every bite!

There goes
the car!

There goes the garage!

The mouth would gobble up EVERYTHING —
including Harvey's house!

And when Harvey would try to find his parents, they would be gone. All he'd be able to find would be their shoes. The shoes would be wet with baby drool.

It was Friday when Harvey's mom came home from the hospital.

His mother held a squirming little creature in her arms. His father looked proud.

"Harvey, come and look at the new baby," his mother said.

"Isn't he cute?" his father said.

So Harvey looked. The baby WAS cute.
He didn't just have a mouth to feed.

He also
had **eyes**
to see.

And **ears**
to hear.

And a **nose**
to sniff.

And **hands**
to clap.

And **legs**
to kick.

And a **belly button** to tickle,
just like any other baby.

"Yes," said Harvey. "He IS cute."

The baby was now a member of the
family. And Harvey felt safe again.

Until dinnertime.

idiom:

a commonly used expression or phrase that means something different from what it appears to mean.

"Another mouth to feed"

is an idiom. It does not mean that there will be a big mouth that keeps growing and growing, like Harvey thought. It means there will be another person around.

MONSTER Street

are published by Picture Window Books — a capstone imprint
151 Good Counsel Drive, P.O. Box 669
Mankato, Minnesota 56002
Visit us at www.capstonepub.com

Printed in the United States of America in North Mankato, Minnesota.
032010
005741CGF10

Library of Congress Cataloging-in-Publication data is available on the Library of Congress website.

ISBN: 978-1-4048-6069-8 (library binding)

Summary: Harvey hears his parents refer to his new sibling as "another mouth to feed." All he can imagine is his new sibling with a mouth that keeps growing and growing.

Cover and interior designed by Bob Lentz